Finding
MICHAEL

GAY SUSPENSE

Dexter Chase

About the Publisher

4Fun Publishing, a member of **BLVNP Incorporated**, 340 S. Lemon #6200, Walnut CA 91789, info@blvnp.com / legal@blvnp.com

NOTE: Due to the highly emotional reaction of some people to works of erotic fiction, any email sent to the above address that contains foul language or religious references is automatically deleted by our anti-spam software and will not be seen. All other communications are welcome.

DISCLAIMER

Please don't be stupid and kill yourself. This book is a work of FICTION. Do not try any new sexual practice that you find in this book. It is fiction and not to be confused with reality. Neither the author nor the publisher or its associates assume any responsibility for any loss, injury, death or legal consequences resulting from acting on the contents in this book. Every character in this book is over 18 years of age. The author's opinions are not to be construed as the opinions of the publisher. The material in this book is for entertainment purposes ONLY. Enjoy.

Finding Michael

Gay Suspense

By: Just Plain Bob

ISBN: 978-1-68030-291-2

Prologue

"You have fouled your body on this infidel my son, but you have done it for the glory of Allah. Now we must make good on our promise to your grandfather and extract the most pain from his father before we dispatch the boy to join the other loathsome creatures of his race. You know what to do?"

"Yes Uncle. We have softened up the mother by sending her photographs of her beloved son as we have made his living conditions less and less palatable. The news is that she is making the father's life hell, as we planned. I have used the time to find ten of my warriors who have been endowed by Allah with the most incredible appendages. These men are truly awesome when naked and erect."

"Good, I wish to see the video before we send it to the she devil and her evil husband."

Abbas was his uncle's favourite nephew, and with no direct male offspring it meant that if he continued as he had done so far, he would inherit that uncle's wealth. The secret he would need to keep forever though was that he didn't consider he had fouled himself making love to this white boy, now languishing in squalid conditions in a hovel at the edge of the palace grounds. Abbas would suffer a terrible death if the uncle knew that he was a true homosexual and had not done it just to gain the confidence of the boy and facilitate the kidnap. The boy, in Abbas's eyes was beautiful but his desire for wealth and power overrode almost everything.

The last photo sent to the mother had shown the boy in a filthy djellaba sitting on the floor in a squalid little hovel his excrement fouling the floor in one corner and his urine running across most of the floor leaving him only a very small space to sit. There was no furniture in the shed and when the boy lay down to sleep part of his body was soaked in that urine.

Today, Michael was pulled from the hovel, stripped naked and taken to a bathroom in the palace. Abbas met him there. Michael fell into his arms and begged him to end the nightmare. He had no idea how long he had been in captivity, the days and nights just ran into one long period of degradation and terror. He was regularly pulled from the hovel and beaten. He had been fed properly for the last few days, but he was still much thinner than his old self and the bruising all over his body front and back was pretty awful. The filth had been constant, the smell so all-encompassing that he didn't notice it until he was pulled out and stripped in the fresh air of the grounds.

"Come, my little one we are going to bathe you and take you to the oasis for a swim, and we will sit and eat dates and fruit."

Michael thought he had been taken to Paradise, it was so long since he had been clean, and now he was able to wallow in fresh steaming hot water for as long as he liked. Abbas used sponges and sweet smelling soaps on him. Stood under a shower at the end of all the pampering, Michael asked Abbas if his ordeal was now over.

"Soon, little one, your father will pay the ransom and we can release you."

"I have not felt your soft lips round my penis for such a long time. Show me that you still love me by drinking my sperm once more."

The blowjob was not very good and Abbas realised how weak Michael was when he had to help him stand.

Michael could hardly believe it. He was given a clean white djellaba and Abbas held his hand as they walked down to the oasis. It was like a Garden of Eden, beautifully manicured lawns leading down to the water's edge. He was surprised to see so many people there, men, women and children. They were all sat around a cleared area that was covered with a plain brown rug. Abbas led Michael to it and they sat talking while a photographer ran a video recorder around them.

"We are going to record a message to send to your parents, so that they know you are well and will dispatch the ransom quickly now that all the negotiations are complete."

Michael smiled into the camera.

"Mum, and Dad, my friend tells me that you are ready to pay the ransom and I can come home. I am so pleased. Life here has been awful, but today Abbas has allowed me to bathe and I am ready to leave here. Please pay the ransom quickly."

The camera panned in to Abbas and he spoke.

"My uncle has decreed that Michael is to pay for the sins of his father. He is to be punished every day until the ransom is paid. I am sorry, I can do nothing about it."

Abbas walked off camera leaving Michael in the centre surrounded by watching women and children as four hefty guards moved in. Two of them took Michael's arms, pulled him to his feet and held them to his side. A third one approached and with no preamble took a knife from his belt, took hold of the neck of Michael's djellaba and slit it neck to floor. Michael looked into the camera showing total terror at this action. The remains of the djellaba was pushed off his shoulders by the guards holding his arms and allowed to fall to the floor. Michael was now stood naked as the camera panned in to take close ups of his genital area. He was turned round and the other two guards took a leg each and spread him very wide before he was forced to bend over and display his anus to the camera. In the sunlight the bruising on his body looked quite awful, Abbas came into the shot again.

"He has such a pretty little virgin hole. It is such a pity that we are not going to allow it to remain that way. Every day until we release him my uncle's personal guards are going to take their pleasure from it."

Michael wasn't a virgin by any means. Abbas had been only one of many lovers that Michael had taken before him, but he had not been sodomised since his kidnapping six months previously.

The camera swung then and ran along a line of ten men. They were all dressed in djellabas and didn't look anything special. The camera returned to Michael and showed him being laid on his back on the rug. His arms and legs were held apart so that he made a star shape. The camera once again showed his whole body. At a nod from Abbas, the legs were pulled further apart and bent up so that his knees were level with his shoulders and spread as wide. The camera zoomed in taking close-ups of his anus, running across his perineum to his testicles and finally his penis that had shrivelled up very small because of his fear.

The first of the ten guards removed his djellaba, eliciting a gasp from the watchers. He was already almost erect and the cock was enormous. The man was very dark skinned, quite a slim build. Only partially erect the penis was at least 12 inches long. He slicked up his hand with spit and fisted himself to a full erection. The monster now was breath-taking. He stood between Michael's legs before kneeling. Michael

He left Harris and immediately hit the speed dial on his sat phone.

"Dan, we're a go. I will be airborne within the hour. All four teams to be on board the Hercules and we'll parachute in an hour before dawn. We have to assume the infirmary for the boy, but team 2 to check the hovel. If we find the boy team 1 &2 take him to the pickup point. Team 3 & 4, destroy with extreme prejudice everything they have time for as they withdraw. No adult male is to survive if they are seen.

The meanest bunch of mercenaries ever put together were ready to go when Mac landed at the forward base where the leased Hercules sat. Every one of them was a qualified parachutist and all were from premier commando outfits. British Royal Marine Commandos and SAS. American Seals and other Special Forces. Israel Mossad Special Attack Operatives.

There were ten more individual men spread round the area that had been the undercover detachment on the ground for the last six months. As a last resort they might be able to help the others if they got into any trouble, otherwise they would leave the country in dribs and drabs the same as they had entered.

"If you find this man Abbas I want him alive, but not seen by anyone when we land."

The extraction would be three Jolly Green Giants. Harris had balked at the cost of hiring them, but they could extract the whole crew in one lift as soon as they got the pickup code. Noisy, but able to land anywhere. Off the coast were two high speed patrol boats. If the helicopter pick up failed they would have to commandeer transport and make for the coast, or try to make it on foot. Every man carried a sat phone and Mac assured them that every means possible would be used to see them safely out of the country.

"Keep your phones switched on. We will keep in touch after extraction until I know that no one is left alive.

Macaulay sat back and thought about the last six months. The day the boy disappeared he really started to earn his keep.

Chapter 1

Macaulay Connors mustered out of the SAS as a half colonel. The youngest in that rank in Special Forces. At 38 years old one would have expected him to remain in the British Services and climb to senior rank, but Mac was abrasive, and tactless. Telling your commanding general that he didn't have a clue and would do the Army a great service by never leaving his office was not the way to secure promotion.

Noel Harris was looking for a first class man to head his security division as he expanded his global media empire. The remit would be to first of all protect his family, well his wife anyway and secondary, protect the personnel and property of Global Media Inc., a multibillion dollar monstrosity that had so many tentacles in to businesses throughout the world that the IRS and tax authorities around the world had given up trying to discover how much tax the enterprise should pay, and accepted the pittance that was offered.

The family consisted of a trophy wife and one son. Michael had proved a big disappointment to him. Instead of a young man that he would groom to take over his empire he had bred a pussy, in his mind.

Michael had been born with the gentle personality of his mother. He grew up a sturdy and healthy child. His loves were music and birds, yes the two legged kind, but all of Michael's loves had feathers. From an early age he had developed a beautiful aviary in the yard of the family's main home in Connecticut. Inside the house was a music room where he could indulge his other love, the piano. By the time he had reached his early teens it had become obvious that this boy could become a concert pianist if he wished, he didn't. Michael was going to be an ornithologist. Noel was almost beside himself with anger almost every time he saw his son and heard how determined he was to study for his dream.

"What about the business? One day you will inherit a company worth billions of dollars. Have you no interest in learning about it, and how to run it?

Michael didn't like to upset his father, he would so have loved the odd cuddle from this man, and encouragement to follow his dream, but all he could do was be honest.

"I'm sorry Sir, I want to study ornithology."

Maria Harris was the only person that could keep Noel in line with regard to his son. He loved her with a ferocity that brooked no compromise in people's dealings with her. No expense she incurred was ever questioned, as against Michael who he would have kept in rags rather than spend a cent on him. Maria was his only extravagance. Despite his billions, Noel Harris was so incredibly mean it almost beggared belief. He would go to extraordinary lengths to save a few cents. Where possible he employed people from third world countries who would work for starvation wages. The only extravagance he allowed was in the employment of his executives. He knew that to make his billions he needed top men in his board rooms, but even that he begrudged.

The exception to this philosophy was his head of security. Changed frequently because for the money he was willing to pay he couldn't get the quality he needed. All of that changed when an attempted kidnap of his wife was foiled by luck rather than his security department.

Noel started his hunt then for a first class replacement. His English newspapers had covered the daring deeds carried out by British Special Forces in war zones and Macaulay Connors name appeared too often to be ignored. The man had a Military Cross and two bars, absolutely unheard of, but he was a totally dedicated soldier of incredible perception and ability in tight situations. When the man resigned his commission because he couldn't stand the incompetence of his commanders any longer, it made headlines, and Noel flew him out to New York, economy of course, for a job interview.

"Mr. Connors, I need a security chief for my worldwide operations, and I need my family protected."

Macaulay asked to see the extent of the domain that he would protect. The sheer scale of it would have put off most men that wanted to do a first class job. Noel's previous chiefs had done it for the money that although not much, was higher than their abilities warranted. Mac's exploration took several hours, which didn't impress Noel. He expected the man to just jump at the chance of getting such a prestigious job. When he told Noel's secretary that he was ready to continue the interview, Noel kept him waiting almost an hour.

"I am ready to listen to your proposals for my terms and conditions. Mr. Harris."

Noel had paid his previous security chief a miserable $100,000 a year with minimal perks or expenses. So he thought that doubling it would look very good. He laid them out for Mac who looked shocked. Noel thought it was because of his generosity. Eventually Mac laughed as he stood up to leave.

"Mr. Harris, we aren't even playing in the same ball park with that offer."

He started to walk out when Noel stopped him by asking him what he expected. Mac turned to answer.

"I would expect to start on a base salary of $1,000,000 per year. Terms and conditions to add to that."

"Don't be ridiculous man that is the kind of money I pay senior executives."

"I don't know what you think your head of security is Mr. Harris, but my guess is that a competent one is probably worth more than one of your senior executives, and believe me, I am a competent one."

Mac turned again and left. Back in England, he thought he would take a holiday before looking for a new job, but that wasn't going to happen. The attempted kidnap of Noel Harris's wife had a major security leak added to it costing the company millions and Noel, after further thought realised he needed this man.. Mac received a call from Noel Harris's personal assistant.

"Colonel Connors. I am Mr. Harris's P.A. He has asked me to get in touch with you concerning the senior executive position he offered you."

Mac couldn't help himself, he laughed before replying.

"I'm sorry you must have a wrong number. Mr. Harris offered me the job of head of security on the salary of a junior manager."

There was embarrassed harrumphing on the other end of the line before the man got his act together.

"Mr. Harris has realised how unrealistic his offer was. He has increased his base salary offer to the $1,000,000 you asked for. He would appreciate if you would let him know what additional expenses your employment would incur."

Mac thought he could have some fun here.

"If you will let me have your email address, I will get everything on paper and let you have it by the end of the week."

It was quite obvious the man had expected an immediate answer and took some convincing that it would take Mac several days to make sure the contract he was proposing was properly drafted. The end result was a package that made Noel Harris explode.

Pension rights and expenses were bad enough, but when Mac also wanted an executive jet to be made available to him 24/7, with his own choice of crew, a specially trained team of ten operatives all at top salaries, and complete control of every aspect of security, he went puce and his secretary thought he was going to have a heart attack. The end result though, was that Mac was invited back for a second interview and was given a first class return ticket.

Noel tried to wheedle the terms and conditions down, but Mac talked them up.

"The executive jet will have to be an intercontinental one. I imagine that limits us a little. A Gulfstream would probably be the only serious choice."

Noel made it clear that his own personal jet was a Gulfstream, did Mac really consider he was worth the same as the President of the company.

"Certainly, because if your security continues to deteriorate someone is going to make sure you don't have a company."

Harris thought about some of the security breaches that had already taken place because of sloppy management in that field, and how much they had cost him. In the scheme of things he realised that if Mac was really good he would save the company much more than he was going to cost him, most of which would be a tax right off anyway.

"Very well Mr. Connors, I am prepared to offer you the contract as you have laid it out, but only for one year."

"Agreed, but with an additional clause that after one year, if you renew it will be for five years with full payment of salary for the whole of that period if you decide to dispense with my services mid contract."

Mac had a full military pension and extensive investments having never spent very much of his salary. If he was going to take a job it was going to be a dream one, or he wouldn't work, so Noel Harris had no choice if he wanted Mac's services. The contract was signed and Mac agreed to start work immediately.

"I need to return to the UK, close up my house and pack my kit to return here. I presume there will be appropriate company accommodation available to me here and in all company locations."

There was, but even giving Mac that was done with poor grace.

Mac spent the first week in his new job exhaustively researching the profiles of all security managers at the company locations, and then all of their subordinates. Finally, the contracts of all of them. Next was a meeting with Noel.

"I am going to sack six of your senior security managers, and 23 other security staff around the world. They are, to put it mildly, a joke. To get the level of expertise I need to properly protect your interests I am going to need to jump their pay scales. That isn't part of our agreement so I need you to tell me how high I can go with each grade. I'll produce a list with my recommendations and you can let me have it back with any adjustments and comments you want to make. Does that sound reasonable?"

Noel could see problems, just taking a quick look at what Mac wanted. Problems there were, but Mac got about 80% of what he had put on paper, meaning that he got 100% of what he really wanted.

The next meeting was just a niggle to Noel.

"I need to go out to the residence, Sir, and see the set up there. I would appreciate if you were there and your wife and son."

Noel was furious at the end of that meeting when he realised how quickly Mac had taken to Michael. The boy was in his last semester before going on to college and he chatted with an obviously interested Mac, for ages.

"I know this is going to appear to be an invasion of your privacy, Michael, and you Mrs. Harris, but I believe you should have personal security round the clock. The last kidnap attempt nearly succeeded. I can't allow that to happen again on my watch."

Noel was thinking dollars and cents and objected.

"I don't know how much worth you attach to your wife and son, Sir, but I won't compromise in protecting the assets that you have entrusted to me. That is my minimum requirement. If you want to take them out of my sphere of responsibility I have no objection to you varying my contract."

Maria's look at Noel was enough.

"No, go ahead, they have to be the highest priority."

Of course what he would like to have done was exclude his son from the package, the boy was useless as far as he was concerned.

"Good, I would like to have a private meeting with your wife and son separately to ascertain their life style and movements."

Maria was easy to deal with at that meeting. She was a very open lady with a lifestyle that was as public as one could wish. Michael was different. Mac could sense that he was holding back on the details of his movements that he was telling Mac.

"Michael, I am not here to judge whether what you do is good bad or indifferent, and your security detail will be the same, but for me to protect you properly I need to know the details of your life, whatever nasties or otherwise there may be in them so that I can tailor your protection to it."

"Will you have to tell dad what I tell you?"

Ah, secrets time.

"I don't have client/lawyer, or doctor/patient laws to abide by, but I promise you that anything you tell me remains between the two of us except as I may use it to protect you."

Mac liked this boy. He was 17 years old, soon to be 18 and off to college, but he had obviously led a sheltered life and was quite naïve and immature. On the subject of music or birds he was very lucid and a confident speaker. For the rest he was shy and unsure of himself. He looked into Mac's eyes, and blushing he spouted out.

"I'm gay, and neither of my parents know. When I go out in the evenings, I'm not going to friends' houses, I am meeting lovers or cruising for them."

Mac probed more and realised that Michael would be an easy target for a kidnap attempt, and he was surprised that hadn't already happened. Maybe it was because he was never seen with his father and Noel never talked about him.

"I'm sorry, Michael, but we have to change this routine a little. When you have a regular boyfriend we can protect you quite easily with co-operation from both of you, but when you are making casual pickups that is fraught with danger and more difficult to cover. Let me think about this. I presume you drive yourself with no security detail."

Michael nodded, looking a little frightened now that he had told someone. Mac could see it. He put a hand on Michael's shoulder and speaking quite softly told him.

"I like you Mike and I look after people I like. I think you are a good son and you shouldn't let your sexuality make you feel bad."

"But I know you are a war hero and a Special Forces operative in your country's Special Air Service. How can you like a little queer boy?"

"Do you think that being gay defines who you are?"

Mike looked a little bemused, shook his head and having thought about it blurted out, "No, of course not."

"No, I don't either. I had openly gay men in some of my units and they were as good as my straight ones. Gay was what they were, not who they were. Their personalities were as diverse as their straight comrades. Besides being gay, what they were, were first class soldiers. You can be gay and a first class anything you put your mind to."

"Thank you Mac. At the moment I have a regular lover. He is from the Middle East and he is older than me. I think I am falling in love with him, he is so good to me. We meet in his apartment as often as I can get away."

Trying not to jump to conclusions Mac immediately had a picture in his mind. Mike he assumed was passive in this relationship and the Middle Eastern man was much more mature and worldly. Mac needed to get details of this guy and make sure he was on the level.

It turned out that the man was mid-20s, studying at university close to where Michael lived. He was not a serious student, turning up for few of his lectures. Finding details of his family proved very difficult and Mac never found out what he needed before action lost him Michael. During that time he had Michael followed everywhere. At his lover's apartment, the operative sat outside in his car. Mac wasn't happy with the arrangement but he allowed it when the man objected to an operative being in the apartment because Michael had been seeing this man for months before he came on the scene.

'If something was going to happen it would surely have happened by now', was Mac's thought which eased his disquiet.

When Mac wasn't globetrotting to all the different locations, he spent more time than was strictly necessary at the Harris mansion, and he realised the reason was that his affection for Michael was growing. The boy was so full of joy when taking part in his activities, practising piano, studying ornithological information.

Mac's pleasure at being shown all of this and played to frequently in the music room made him realise how much he missed not having a family. Maria noticed this and was worried about Mac's agenda. Outspoken lady, she asked Mac to join her in the study at the house one day.

"Mac, you spend much more time with Michael than is necessary for your job. Would you like to tell me why?"

Mac blushed, not something he did very often.

"Mrs Harris, I never married and of course I have no children. Since meeting Michael I have realised how much I would have liked to have a son like him. He is a total joy to me, being around him relaxes me so much it amazes me. I have come to realise that I want to protect him even more than I do at the moment, and if his father's attitude to him was different I could. I am not gay and I don't have any ulterior motives where he is concerned, except my desire to be his friend, despite the 20 year difference in age."

"But you know Michael is gay, I presume."

Mac was surprised, and it showed.

"I think I have known for years, Mac. His father would as well if he cared to look. His liaisons must make life difficult for you trying to protect him."

Mac nodded and told Maria his feelings on the subject.

"If he were able to be open with his father, boyfriends could come here, he could see them openly, all of this would make it easier for us to protect him. As it is, whenever he sees his current lover we have to leave him without immediate cover while he is in the guy's apartment."

"Thank you for being honest with me Mac. Please, in future will you call me Maria?"

Mac smiled, "I'd like that."

During the next few months, Michael and Mac drew closer together making it easy for Mac to discover more about him, and the boyfriend, but there was still a mystery about the family of this mystery lover.

Chapter 2

Mac had been in the job for more than six months when Noel decided to have an audit carried out to see how effective he had been. The figures astounded him. Mac's security makeover had been so good that money lost from security breaches in the last six months was the lowest ever. The savings amounted to millions, more than covering the total cost of security. Noel was never going to like Mac, he didn't like his military bearing, his independence, or his ability to remain totally uninfluenced by the boss. But, he did like to see the savings on the bottom line. Another thing he didn't like was how close he had become with his son, and his wife. Maria quite patently admired Mac and with his son he felt it went further. He talked about Mac as though he were a friend.

"Just remember, Michael, Connors is just an employee, you should keep him at arm's length and treat him like any other member of staff."

Michael just dropped his head and mumbled a, 'Yes Sir.'

Noel didn't care that he was never called dad, was never addressed at all in fact. Michael only spoke to him to answer questions. Those were few and far between because his interests were not his father's.

Michael realised that with regard to human interaction there were only three in his life that he cared about. His mother, Mac and Abbas, his lover. There were no real friends at school. Most were either afraid of his father's money and power, or were sycophants just toadying up to him because of that. It made for a slightly lonely boy.

Lying in the arms of Abbas one evening he let these thoughts out. They had made love on the sofa in the lounge, Michael just loved the feel of Abbas's giant cock sliding in and out of his love chute. He had soon gotten used to its girth when they first became lovers. Abbas had taken a picture of this particular session on his blackberry. They had joked about it until Michael had gotten serious.

"I love you Abbas. When I am older and independent of my father's wealth I want us to live together like man and wife. I want to look after you and show you how much I have come to love you."

Looking at the photo once Abbas had downloaded it and printed it, he told Michael his thoughts.

"Well, you are certainly pretty enough for me to take you as my wife, but look at your legs, they are much too hairy."

Michael studied the picture as well. He could see that above the waist he was quite attractive. His short black hair looked good and never needed much attention, he thought his face was elfin looking which he knew pleased Abbas, so no problem there. The torso was smooth and pale with good muscle definition, well, reasonable. After all, he wasn't an athlete. The cock didn't matter because Abbas only ever played with it, he never blew it or let Michael take the active roll. Even so it was a decent length and shape. Perhaps his balls were a little small, but they did loosen up when Abbas played.

Laughing and snuggling in close to Abbas, Michael replied.

"That's alright we can shave them. You can do anything you like to me. You know I will still love you."

Abbas felt just a twinge of guilt, and then it was gone as he thought about what the prize would be if he carried off the plan for this little rich white boy. He did enjoy burying his large tool in the little boy ass, it was better than a woman's hole, whichever one you used. Boys were so much more exciting, and in the case of Michael, never said no, never complained no matter how many times he wanted to fuck in the few hours they had together. He wondered if he would be able to indulge when Michael was a prisoner in his uncle's compound.

The term ended, Michael celebrated his eighteenth birthday and his mother told him he could travel round Europe. Mac was mortified. How on earth was he going to protect the boy there? He was sure Harris would balk at the expense of security cover for him.

Thanks to Maria a compromise was reached and Michael had some cover, but Mac would have been happier if he had found out as much as he wanted to about Abbas who was going with him. His unease about this Middle Eastern man just kept growing, but he had been Michael's lover for more than six months and nothing had happened. Mac detailed one of his most trusted men to the job.

"Harry, I'm not happy with this, but you are going to be on duty all the time you are away. No relief, no days off. I don't trust Michael's companion so we aren't going to tell either of them that you are in attendance."

Harry was, like Mac, multi-lingual and a master of disguise. It was very unlikely that his cover would ever be blown.

Michael's itinerary was settled with Mac emphasising that he should stick to it, without going into detail. He didn't want Michael to know that they had to book Harry's tickets to coincide with Michael's.

Reluctantly, Mac took Michael and Abbas to the airport.

"You have your sat 'phone. Speed dial 1 is direct to my cell. That is on 24/7, don't hesitate to call me if you need to, day or night. I want you to call your mother and talk to her frequently as well. She is going to miss you."

Michael assured Mac he would.

The boy wasn't even his son, but he felt a great sense of loss knowing that he wouldn't be seeing him for a month.

A small crisis in South Africa meant he had to fly there and for a week, Mac was absorbed in putting it right. Just as he thought it would be safe to return to the head office, his phone rang, it was Harry.

"I've got a problem Mac. Michael and his boyfriend got on a private jet a few minutes ago. I can't follow them."

"Alright Harry. Find out from air traffic where the jet is flying to. Find a local charter company that will fly you to the same destination and give me their phone number, we'll get you there only a little while behind them. I'll call Michael and find out what is going on."

Mac didn't like it. He had a very nasty feeling in his mind about this. He called Michael's sat phone.

"Oh, hi Mac."

"Hi yourself. Now, you've deviated from your plan. Where are you going?"

"How on earth did you know?"

"Never mind that, where are you going?"

"Oh, Abbas thought I might like to see the Acropolis so we are going to Athens."

No point in making a big deal about it, he couldn't influence anything yet.

"Ok, give me a call when you land, and tell me where you are staying."

Harry got to him with the same information and a charter company. Mac paid for an immediate charter to Athens in a Lear jet. Harry called Mac within a few minutes of landing at Athens Airport.

"The kid's plane hasn't landed. I talked to air traffic and they say that the jet cancelled its flight plan but didn't file an alternative."

"Stay put, Harry, try to find out where the damn thing went. I'll call you when I know anything."

Using all the leverage that the use of the Global Media name could apply, Michael's jet had disappeared from the radar and no one knew where. No one knew anything. The registration number on the fuselage was a false one.

Mac flew home, he would be more effective at company HQ with their global communications network. He went straight to the house to see Maria. She was so distraught that Mac called a doctor and had her sedated.

'Where the fuck is her husband,' was Mac's thought. He found him in the offices conducting business as usual. Mac stormed into Noel's office.

"You do know that your son has been kidnapped and your wife is so distraught I have had to get a doctor in to sedate her."

Showing virtually no concern Noel replied.

"What were you doing at the house and yes I know my son is missing, but that is why I pay you, find him."

Mac was left speechless by the callous attitude of the man. He left and went into the communications centre. He had already formulated the first stage of his plan by the time he got there. He spoke to general managers of every office Global had anywhere in the world, rousting them out of bed where necessary.

"I want you all to make it a first priority. All of your security staff are to be out on the streets listening for news about an abduction of the Harris boy. I expect some feedback within 24 hours."

There was mumblings of dissent. Did the boss know, etc.

"The missing boy is the boss's only son. How long do you think you will hold your job if you don't co-operate?"

'Forever,' was the sick thought that followed that. Then it was back to the boss to get the second part of his plan moving.

"I want $1,000,000 transferred into my personal account immediately. I'm sending ten of my best men into the areas that I think Michael might have been taken. If they need it I want them to have adequate funds. They may not need any of it but I can't risk losing him for the sake of a few dollars."

Wrong thing to say, 'a few dollars it wasn't', in Harris's mind "You are so fond of him, you put up the million."

"Very well, I'll tell Mrs. Harris why I have just resigned before I leave for London."

That caused a jolt. His wife would divorce him and take him to court for billions in a divorce case and he would be losing a man that had already saved him millions.

"Oh very well, but I want every cent of it accounted for."

Ten master undercover operatives were in the Middle East within 24 hours with credit cards each of which had a $100,000 limit on it.

All that they could do now was sit and wait.

Absolutely no contact was made for a month, none of Mac's men had heard a whisper. The jet had not re-appeared either. Mrs. Harris was being sedated regularly as she gradually came apart at the seams, and Noel carried on as usual never once asking Mac how the investigation was going.

After that month, Noel received one photograph a week as an attachment to an email. The first one was the picture taken by Abbas with his cock halfway up Michael's ass. There was no possibility of thinking it was an unwanted penetration. The look on Michael's face was pure pleasure. Noel stormed into Mac's office.

"Did you know my son was a screaming queen? I might have guessed the useless little shit."

Wrong thing to say to Mac who was feeling the loss.

"Yes I knew that Michael was gay. If you ever talk to me again about your son using that tone and that kind of language I'll throw you out of this window."

They were on the 22nd. Floor.

"You're fired you arrogant bastard. Who the fuck do you think you are talking to?"

Mac didn't say a word. He picked up his briefcase. Put his laptop in it, slid a few personal possessions into it, including a photo of Michael and his mother that Noel didn't even know he had. He locked it, and walked passed Noel without making eye contact. He knew that if he did he would hit the man and he needed his freedom to continue looking for Mike.

He was already in the lift before Noel got his act together. The last thing he had expected was Mac walking without saying a word.

Mac drove straight out to the estate to see Maria.

"I'm sorry Maria, your husband has just found out that Michael is gay. He received a photo of Michael with his lover's penis protruding from his ass. He sacked me on the spot for failing to tell him. My men are still in place with substantial funds so I'll continue to monitor them from my own communications set up when I am back in England. I don't have the funds or facilities to continue at my present level out here."

No better tonic could have been devised to bring her out of her depression. Despite the lack of progress, Maria was convinced that if she was ever to see her son again it would be because of this man. She picked up a telephone and called her husband's office.

"I want you to re-instate Mac this minute, give him full co-operation in his bid to rescue my son, and to immediately forward to Mac and myself any future correspondence, photos, or whatever, including the present one. If you don't do all those things Noel, I'll file for divorce in the morning and demand a settlement of 10 billion dollars, which is less than half your fortune so I know I'll get it. I am handing the phone to Mac, now."

Mac put the phone to his ear but said nothing as he tried to envisage 10 billion.

"You've got your job back you bastard, but watch your back from now on."

Then he hung up.

"I guess I'd better get back to the office before I get the sack again."

Maria then did completely the unexpected. She threw herself into Mac's arms.

"We are going to get him back Mac, aren't we?"

He held her close revelling in the feel of this woman.

"Yes we'll get him back, I swear it."

Driving back into town he mused, *'now all I have to do is find him alive.'*

The photo wasn't very helpful. Mac knew it had been taken in Abbas's apartment so it was a month old at least. He looked at it for ages thinking that Michael was beautiful. Not beautiful like his mother, but in a masculine way.

"I have to save you boy, for both our sakes. I'll be lost without you now."

Chapter 3

The pictures came now, regularly one per week, no note with them and no traceable email address. There were no more pornographic ones. In each of them Michael was dressed either in a djellaba or was naked to the waist in a filthy pair of boxer shorts. He was always in the hovel that they came to recognize and he looked thinner and more drawn facially in each one. Where he was naked to the waist the bruises all over his body could be seen. In only one of them was his face marked. He had a black eye. The djellaba became filthier as did the boxers. It was obvious he was never bathed or his clothes washed. Occasionally a metal bowl was shown in the pictures with some filthy glutinous mess in it. Presumably his food. There was no furniture in the room so it was assumed he slept on the floor. It was six months before the full level of his degradation was seen. A flood light was brought in for one of the photographs and they could see the pile of excrement in the corner and the pools of urine all over the floor. That was the photo that should have broken Maria Harris and sent her to the mental hospital, but it did the reverse. She spent almost every waking hour dogging Mac's footsteps, goading him into thinking of new avenues that he could explore. He was moving his men around the Middle East all the time hoping for a clue. He delved into all of Noel's business dealings to find a link to someone who he had done down as he acquired all his business interests. Nothing, and most frustrating of all, nothing new on Abbas, whatever his other name was.

The break when it came surprised the hell out of Mac. It came from one of his old unit officers. Tommy O'Rourke was from Northern Ireland. He had mustered out just after Mac. He had been in a bar in East Belfast one night and had heard two men talking. They were ex-IRA and they were discussing the abduction of the teenage son of Global Media's boss. Tommy knew that Mac had gone there, and had offered him a job when he finished his time. He had not taken Mac up on it, but held his old boss in high regard, so he listened.

"The old Emir would go crazy if he knew what his younger brother was doing. He has been courting the Western governments for years hoping for inward investment so that he can bring his people into the 21st. Century. They have all the oil revenue, but because of his terrorist past he can't get the tech support he wants."

Tommy had mulled over that conversation and decided it might be useful to Mac.

"I'd like to speak to Colonel Connors please."

The strong Irish accent almost made the receptionist at Global Media, hang up, she barely understood him. Eventually she put him through to Mac's secretary, who in turn to Mac after he recognised the name.

"Tommy, how are you? What can I do for you? Are you going to take up my job offer now?"

Mac could use someone like Tommy. Not on this operation but there was plenty of opportunity for a skilled undercover man in most of the world where he could work.

Tommy laughed.

"One question at a time, but first the reason for the call. Are you still looking for the Harris boy?"

Mac nearly wet his pants.

"Are you kidding? We are spending a king's ransom keeping operatives in the field looking for clues on this one."

"Do you remember the old Emir who used to support terrorism until we taught him a lesson? You led the raid that reduced his desert palace to a pile of rubble and his stables to a burnt out pile of ash."

Mac laughed, "Yes that was the best bonfire night I ever had. Guy Fawkes would have been proud of me."

"Yes, well the old boy has a viper in his nest. His younger brother is the one that abducted young Harris and is holding him in another desert palace in the Emirate."

"Are you sure, Tommy?"

"No, but that's what I heard last night."

"I'm not going to waste time chattering Tommy. Please keep in touch though because if this pans out I will owe you a debt of gratitude I doubt I'll ever be able to repay."

"You can bet on it Colonel, I'm ready to come back to work now."

Mac put the phone down, picked it up again and spoke to each of his ten bloodhounds in the Middle East.

"I want you into Abu Sheif,, find out everything you can about the younger brother of the Emir. All ten of you are going to be there so be careful not to fall over each other."

Twenty four hours later Mac had so much information coming in he had to use several more security personnel to sift through it and collate it. The piece of info that sealed Mac's thinking on Michael's position was a photo of Abbas taken in the main town a few days after the operation started, with details. Abbas was the nephew and favoured relative of the Emir's younger brother. Mac ordered all operatives to concentrate on this one man. Under no circumstances were they to be discovered tailing him.

"I want to know everything there is to know about any place he goes. If he lives at his uncle's home I want as much information about it as possible."

The ten men went at it in the only manner they knew how with undercover work. They became invisible. Six of them made hides for themselves, spread around the periphery of the palace where Abbas lived with his uncle. The other four wandered round the palace area and the outlying areas looking for escape routes if they became necessary. The first positive report came from one of the operatives on the periphery.

"Mac, there is a broken down hovel at one edge of the palace grounds. Once a day a guard goes down to it with a metal plate." He laughed. "It's a shiny metal plate, which is nice of them. I am assuming food for someone in the hut.

The following day the food was escorted by three guards. The prisoner was brought out, stripped and used as a punch bag by the three. The watcher had a high powered zoom lens on his camera and sent the result, via satellite to Mac.

Mac was torn between jumping for joy and dissolving in tears. It was Michael, but he was a bunch of skin and bone, and he was bruised all over. He looked awful. Mac decided he couldn't show Maria the picture, but he showed Noel.

"I want carte blanche to build a rescue team. I will need a military aircraft to drop paras, I think, and then boats and or helicopters to extract my rescue teams. I can't even begin to give you an end price until I have done some more planning."

Noel was thinking dollars.

"The little shit isn't worth a dollar."

Before he continued he remembered what had happened the last time he had spoken like that. He held his hands up in front of him.

"Alright, alright, just keep the cost down as low as you can."

Mac stormed out before he hit the callous bastard. He telephoned Maria who for a change was at home, instead of in his office.

"I want you to call Lottie and then sit down. Put the phone onto speaker. When you have done that we'll talk."

"What is it Mac? Is it Michael? Is he dead? You swore to me you would save him."

She was getting hysterical so he spoke again.

"I'm going to, very soon, but I need you to do as I tell you first."

Job done. "Lottie is here Mac and I'm sat down."

"All right. I have proof positive that half an hour ago Michael was alive. He doesn't look very well, but he is functioning under his own steam."

Reaction was exactly what he expected. She just disintegrated.

"Lottie, take Mrs. Harris to her bed and make her take one of the sedative tablets. I promise you she will not sack you if you have to force her to take it, whatever she may say. Tell her I need 12 hours to set things in motion and then I will be at the house to tell her everything."

Google earth was invaluable during the next several days as they scoured every possible approach, every possible escape route. His ten men produced attack charts, withdrawal charts, and detailed reports on terrain, transport and finally personnel. Jihadists, women and children, and their location.

The work was exhaustive. There would be no second chance. Troops couldn't be used to storm the palace because that kind of warning would almost certainly guarantee Michael being killed and disposed of the second a gun was fired. Michael's rescue had to be the first thing anyone knew anything was happening.

True to his word, after he had briefed everyone and the wheels had started to turn, Mac drove out to the house. He had to show Maria the picture. She cried, but she also realised that her baby was alive. They would soon build him up again and the bruises would go. A good psychiatrist would hopefully handle the mental side, and she, with Mac's help, would lavish more love on him than he could ever expect.

Yes, Maria now believed that Mac's love for her son was paternal. He would make a good father when she divorced Noel, always provided Mac felt the same as she did.

Intelligence reports kept pouring in from his men while Mac gathered together a bunch of the most evil mercenaries he could find. They were ready to go having carried out extensive training as teams under Mac's guidance. The final pieces of the jigsaw were in place when a greedy defence minister in an African state was persuaded to release three jolly green giants for Mac to use. He put his own pilots into them and had them transported by sea to a drop off point close enough to carry out the task. GPS on the choppers and at least two more with each team. Co-ordinates for the pickup would be agreed when the situation was clear. A civil Hercules was on call at a desert airfield in a neighbouring state. The video of Mike's multiple rape was the go signal. Mac was airborne in the Gulfstream within the hour. He would brief the teams as they flew to the drop point in the Hercules. He would like to have gone in with them but he knew he was needed to co-ordinate the whole operation. He would go in with the choppers for the pickup, he just couldn't stay out of it completely.

Whilst he was winging his way to the Middle East, Mac got the luckiest break he could have wished for. One of the watchers at the palace called him.

"Mac, the boy has been returned to the hovel. He was carried in on a stretcher, and left. When you are ready for the pickup it looks as though the kid will already be in his stretcher ready for you."

Mac very quickly redesigned his plan. Teams 1& 2 would both go to the hovel, bring Michael out and protect him with their lives. Teams 3 & 4 would carry high explosives as well as their personal weapons. Once they were airborne in the Hercules, Mac briefed them.

Teams 1 & 2 were shown the aerial shots containing the hovel.

"The moment you have him make the call. Let's be corny, call that the Eagle has landed." The teams all laughed. "Then you head out to the West. If the chopper pickup fails you are going in the right direction for plan B, rescue launches waiting off the coast. Initial co-ordinates for pickup are these." Mac passed each team member a paper. "If things change we'll convey new ones to you on your sat phones. Any questions?"

Mac looked pointedly at his four team leaders.

"Teams 3 & 4 I expect the sky to look like November 5th. When you get the go ahead."

Mac wanted Michael clear before he set his killer dogs loose.

There was nothing more Mac could do after they had checked their equipment for the nth. time and carried out a last comms check with their sat phones.

"All team deputy leader leave your phones on transmit to my phone. I want to hear as much as possible."

The drop was perfect and Mac was back on the ground with the choppers, ready to go before the attack started.

The silence from the phones had Mac on tenterhooks He heard a crash, and less than a minute later a message.

"The Eagle has landed."

Mac smiled and breathed a sigh of relief. It was five more minutes before the next message.

"I don't think they know we are here, Mac. Team 1 has Michael, stretcher bound. We are heading for the pickup."

"Well done, team 2, split, half to point, half to drag. Team 1 no change. Eagle is prime priority."

Mac looked at the map. Worked out distances and told his pilots.

"Giant 1 & 2, we go in thirty minutes. Giant 1, you pick up Eagle and team 1. Any problem and Giant 2 does it. If there are no problems, team 2 come back in Giant 2, otherwise we call in Giant 3. Both of you return here to drop everyone. All three Giants return to pick up teams 3 & 4."

A Swiss watch never ran as smoothly as the operation. Mac checked out Michael as soon as he was on-board. He was still unconscious but his pulse was strong. The choppers were airborne again in minutes after Michael had been loaded into the Gulfstream with the medical team, and dispatched back to the States. Mac went in Giant 1 to lead in the others for the second pickup. The glow on the horizon from the Sheikh's palace was impressive. The pickup was faultless and within minutes the choppers were on their way back. The reports to Mac were inspiring.

"One of the silly buggers got a bullet wound in his arm, Mac, otherwise no casualties. The rescue was so quiet that we had time to place charges in loads of prime locations. Really sloppy security. They were obviously not expecting any trouble. We sat in a semi-circle about 100 yards from the main building and then blew the charges. It was like watching rats leaving a sinking ship. Head count I would guess at in excess of 100, besides those that died in the blast. We did save one of them for you though. Sean Govern recognized him as he tumbled out of one of the doors and invited him to join us. Answers to the name, Abbas."

Mac wanted to kiss Sean for that. Instead, what he did, was add £10,000 of his own money to Sean's check.

Mac told the boats that they could withdraw as the Hercules took off to return to friendly skies.

Abbas was taken to a secret location by three of Mac's most trusted operatives. He intended to deal with him at his leisure, later.

When he landed back in New York, he went straight to the private clinic that Michael had been taken to.

Maria was sat alongside Michael's bed holding his hand when he walked in. Before he could do or say anything he had an armful of lady burying him in kisses.

"There is nothing I won't do for you for the remainder of my life. Thank you, thank you, thank you."

When he managed to untangle himself, Mac looked at the boy. In a low voice he asked.

"How is he?"

Maria had tears in her eyes as she replied.

"The doctors have put him into an induced coma. They want his body to heal before bringing him back. Oh, Mac, his anus is terribly mutilated. He has had some reconstructive surgery, but it will be a long time before we can be sure how much permanent damage has been done.

His vital signs are all good. Blood tests are being carried out. We can only pray that he is clean."

The more he heard, the more Mac was determined that Abbas would never know peace again on this earth. He sat with Maria for a while and watched Michael.

"Has his father seen him, or even asked after him?"

Maria shook her head. "No, nothing."

When Mac got up to leave he kissed Maria and stroked Michael's cheek.

"Fight for it, Tiger, we have a lot to do when you leave here."

Maria heard and knew what she was going to do.

Mac went straight to Noel's office.

"Your son's rescue was completely successful. I will let you have the final accounting for the cost of the rescue as soon as I can, along with my resignation."

Then he turned and left before Noel could reply.

Back at his own desk, Mac worked through the rescue expenses as fast as he could. The ten operatives that had been infiltrated into Abu Sheif had all contacted Mac to say they were clear. Instruction to all of them was the same.

"Take your fee and transfer the remainder of the money back to my account. You have my thanks and my gratitude for a first class job."

He paid for the boats, the Hercules and the three choppers, plus all the transport charges. The four teams were paid handsomely.

Ten days later, Mac presented Noel with the bill for the rescue of his son. It came to a little over $3,000,000. Noel almost had apoplexy when he saw the bottom line. He spluttered for ages before being able to string a sentence together.

"That's ridiculous, I'm taking it out of your salary." Mac laughed.

"I think you owe me about two weeks money, you can have it. My desk will be clear in ten minutes and I'll be clear of this complex a few minutes later. My resignation is on my desk."

Noel Harris sat down with a thump. That bastard had spent his money like water to rescue a useless little queer. He was furious and his week didn't improve.

Chapter 4

The moment Mac told Maria that he had resigned from Global she phoned her lawyer and told him to serve the divorce papers on her husband. Then she talked to Mac.

"I hope you are going to stay on here to be near Michael."

Mac beamed, "Just try to stop me. I need to get out of the company flat before your husband decides to invade it and throw my gear out on the street, and then find somewhere to stay.

Maria quickly wrote an address down and passed it to him.

"I will call the concierge and ask him to give you a set of keys and show you to an apartment I own. You can stay there as long as you like, Mac."

Company flat cleared, but only just in time. Mac was about to leave with his last case when two of Noel's fixers walked in. They tried to stop Mac taking his case with him. It was sometime before they were conscious and operating properly again.

The apartment that Mac was shown into by the concierge took Mac's breath away. Luxury in no way described it. Only a top flight interior designer could have produced something like this. No expense had been spared. Mac laughed, he just knew that Noel had paid for it but had nothing to do with decorating and furnishing it.

All organized and Mac was back in the clinic to see Michael. He told the doctors who he was, what his interest was in Maria and Michael before asking for a totally truthful account of what had been done for Michael, what more they could do, how long it was likely to take, and what were the chances of Michael making a full physical and mental recovery.

"We can't possibly tell you that Mr. Connors, we haven't even told Mrs. Harris a lot of it."

"I guessed that. Now let me tell you what is going to happen. If you don't give me the information now, I am going to call back some of the jackals I used to rescue Michael and I am going to make your lives so terrifyingly horrendous that you will pray to be sent to hell which will look like Paradise by the time I have finished. I will include your families as well."

The team of doctors looked at Mac, looked at each other, and the chief surgeon spoke.

"You had better sit down, this will take some time."

Mac made himself comfortable and unbeknown to the doctors switched on a recording device he had in his pocket. The microphone was a badge on the lapel of his jacket. The information that unfolded turned Mac's usual healthy tan a sickly yellow color.

"Michael's anus and anal passage first. The lower part of Michael's large intestine has been destroyed completely. We cut it out and hopefully the finished article when all the stitches dissolve and the swelling subsides will not give him any problems. The sphincter muscle is such a mess we haven't yet touched it. We are waiting for the swelling to subside and hope we can repair it, but our prognosis is that he will almost certainly need to be fitted with a catheter for the remainder of his life, or wear a nappy, like a child. The anus itself we are treating to stop any infection taking hold and after we have worked on the sphincter we will try to sow that up again. The internal tissue is likely to leave severe scarring as it heals, but although it is very delicate membrane it could heal well because the boy is young. Body wise, the beatings have been quite severe and internal organs are bruised quite badly. We are cleaning his blood artificially while we decide whether to carry out a liver transplant or hope it starts to heal itself. His throat is also badly damaged, we are assuming that the objects that ruined his anus have been used on his mouth as well. We have removed his tonsils. We are hoping that his vocal chords are not damaged but we have to consider the idea that he may never speak again. The induced coma is because we think that his present physical state is so poor and there is so much pain that the alternative would be to turn him into a zombie keeping the pain at an acceptable level."

"How long before you will consider bringing him out of his coma?"

The doctors looked at each other and shrugged.

"Mr. Connors. We don't want to sound too pessimistic, but please don't look at less than a year. The damage is so extensive we are actually surprised he survived."

Mac wanted to cry, this beautiful boy was about to salvage his emotional sanity before he was kidnapped, now he might be a partial invalid unable to communicate with him in a normal way.

'Abbas is going to receive the same treatment, only more so,' was Mac's thought as he staggered out of the clinic.

The next morning, Mac woke up in a police cell feeling worse than he had ever done in his life before. The desk sergeant filled him in on what he knew as he gave Mac his property, collected the fine for being drunk and disorderly and warned him against repeating the previous night's action. Apparently he had simply walked out of the clinic, walked into a bar and worked his way through two fifths of bourbon. Not bad for a guy who normally drank a maximum of two shots, if he drank at all.

He went back to the apartment, showered and shaved. He drank several cups of coffee while he played the tape he had recorded and cried like a baby for the son that he loved that wasn't even his.

Back at the clinic he took Maria to the cafeteria and sat her in a quiet corner.

"The doctors are going to keep Michael in an induced coma while his body heals. We can do nothing directly to help him. If you spent a couple of hours a day in here talking to him, that is about as useful as you can be. With your permission I'm going to do the same. The remainder of your day should be spent sorting out your life so that when Michael is brought back to us you can devote all of your time to him. I want you to employ me as your security chief as well. I'm not greedy, $1 per year will do to make the contract legal, but I will need to be funded for personnel to protect you."

Maria agreed. Noel would have to keep her funded until the divorce was final. The initial agreement was that Maria keep the house and her allowance would be sufficient to maintain her life style and pay staff. An afterthought, but one that she forced through with her lawyer's help was that Mac's Gulfstream and his crew would be handed over to her.

"Mac, I am going for 50% of his fortune, well 10 billion anyway. Whatever I get will almost certainly be stock not cash so I am going to try to get control of companies that I think I can run myself. I did after all, get the same degree in business management that Noel got. I will need an organization the same as Noel so I want you as my chief of security. After the settlement we can negotiate a proper contract."

What she wasn't telling Mac was that the contract she was going to angle for was a marriage contract.

With everything in place, Mac took time off to attend to Abbas. He was presently being kept in a wood shed on a wilderness property Mac had acquired. The cabin was pleasant enough with its own water supply and generator. The guards drove into the nearest town for their food and drink. Abbas was kept in the same conditions as Michael had been. Mac picked up some low life's from a rundown part of the city. He offered them $1,000 each for two days work.

"To qualify for the pay you must have more than 9 inches between your legs and be prepared to fuck a male arse."

Not a problem, most of these guys would fuck anything for $10 bucks, never mind $1,000.

When he had his numbers he transported them out to the cabin. He told his men what was going to happen. Abbas was brought out from his hovel and stripped, given a bar of carbolic soap and shown to an outside shower. Cold water only, but at least he was clean at the end.

"Michael is alive, in a coma at the moment, but when he comes back to us he is almost certain to be an invalid. I love that boy like a father would so you can imagine what is going to happen to you. These men are here to entertain you for the day."

Mac had briefed the men on the drive to the cabin. It kept their minds occupied as they were kept blindfolded.

"When you are given the creature, the requirements are that you fuck his face and his arse as often as you like until you can't get erections. When you are all sated you can use him as a punch bag, but I don't want him damaged so that we can't use him again."

Mac and his two men had a ring side seat watching the action, a lot of it mirroring what had happened to Michael in that last video.

Mac allowed them free rein for two days before he called a halt and drove them back to New York, thank them and gave them $1,000 each in crisp new notes.

"Thank you guys. The telephone number on the wrapper is for you to use if you would like to do the same again one month today."

The eight men thought that was great. When you had nothing, a thousand dollars a month looked like a fortune.

Abbas was kept without toilet facilities and offered food that was as revolting as Michael's had been. He was tended to medically so that he could be used again, and again, and again. After six months, that coincided with Michael's time in captivity the men were allowed three days with him and then he was just thrown back into the hovel and left. The two operatives were told to leave him until he was dead and then to burn the hovel to the ground and leave no trace of human remains.

Maria's divorce case had been heard and she got her 10 billion. The rather drawn out conclusion to that was agreeing what companies she would take over. Mac had been taken on as a proper security chief and had shuffled personnel around to make sure that the ones in Maria's companies were the best there were.

Both of them spent a couple of hours a day talking to Michael and in Mac's case getting a full briefing on his health every week. After six months the lead consultant sat both Maria and Mac down to give them an in depth assessment of Michael's condition and the prognosis.

"We have done everything we think possible now as far as surgery is concerned. We are pleased with everything we can see except the sphincter. That is an ongoing work for his body to handle, but we are reasonably confident that it will function again, how efficiently we aren't sure. The bruising of his internal organs has cleared and they all appear to be functioning quite efficiently. We are delighted with his liver function and no more dialysis is contemplated. His throat looks totally normal now, but we won't know until we bring him out of his coma whether he will be able to speak or not. With your permission Mrs. Harris we want to bring him back over the next month."

Maria looked at Mac. The anguished look on her face said much more than words could. Mac took her in his arms and whispered to her.

"It is earlier than we expected. That must be a good sign, and now we both have the time to spend with him to help his convalescence."

Mac had employed Tommy O'Rourke as soon as he left Global and had trained him to be his deputy as he had been in the SAS. There were no huge problems in the security business of Maria's companies so he could take time out for Michael.

The first indication that Michael was re-joining the world was when Maria felt him squeeze her hand as she was talking to him. Then he opened his eyes and smiled at his mother.

"Hello Mum," came out a little raspy, but the words turned Maria to jelly and she just burst into tears.

"Oh Michael, I love you so much."

"I love you too," and then he was asleep. Maria summoned the doctor and told him everything. He was delighted.

"Mrs. Harris I think we have won. The boy must have incredible inner strength to have come so far much quicker than we anticipated, and with much less permanent damage. We must still take it very gently so please don't tire him when he wakes again, and don't expect him to do anything unless we tell you it is ok."

Maria phoned Mac, and told him, he was in the clinic almost before she had put the phone down. He sat down on the other side of the bed to Maria and took Michael's other hand. In a very soft voice he spoke to the boy he had grown to love.

"Hiya Tiger, I knew you would come through for me. Now you think about all the things we are going to do together when you are fit again."

He looked at Maria and she smiled at him as she nodded her head.

Michael stirred and squeezed Mac's hand with some strength.

"Hello Mac, I knew you would be here. I've felt your strength. Thank you."

Mac cried then, cried like he hadn't since he was a baby. Out of the sobbing came words that Michael had only dreamed of.

"I love you Mike, I'm going to look after you for the rest of my life."

Maria knew then that tonight she would accept Mac's proposal of marriage.

The doctors came and checked the boy thoroughly while he was still awake. They gave him his antibiotics orally for the first time, and a draft that would send him into a relaxed and healing sleep.

Mac took Maria out to a celebration dinner from which she emerged with a beautiful diamond engagement ring.

Michael was in hospital for another two months gradually checking all his functions. The most important one and the funniest was when his sense of humour shone through.

Mac and he were alone, Maria attending to business. Mike looked at Mac with a little boy look and spoke.

"Please Daddy, can I leave this nappy off now, I haven't pooped in it for days," then he giggled.

"Please Mac, I guess my sphincter must be ok, I really can control my bowel movements now and I'm nearly nineteen, I shouldn't have to wear nappies."

The two of them giggled and Mac, looking resigned replied.

"Ok, I'll take it off for you."

Starting to remove Michael's bedclothes, expecting the boy to try to stop him, he was only offering as a joke and was shocked at the unexpected reply.

"I want you to, Mac. You have only seen my body when it was barely human, now I want you to see me nearly normal. What I am now is all down to you, I would be dead otherwise. I know everything about my six months in captivity and what you did to find me and get me out. You're going to be my dad now as well so it is only right you see all of your son."

Mac sat on the bed and touched Mike's cheek.

"I know you're a gay man, but are you sure about this?"

Mike smiled a shy smile.

"Yes, I'm sure, I planned it this way. I love you Mac, I want you to see all of me, to make sure I'm worthy of your love in body, and when I am well, in mind as well."

Slowly, Mac rolled down the bedclothes and looked at this boy that he loved. He looked good. His skin was clear, no blemishes anywhere. He hoped the back view was the same. He undid the pin on the adult nappy and gently pulled it clear. Mike raised his bottom to facilitate the removal displaying his groin area unashamedly.

Lying naked, Mike looked into Mac's eyes showing the apprehension he felt. He wanted this man's approval more than anything else in the world.

"You are a beautiful young man Mike. You look perfect to me."

Mike smiled and rolled over.

"You had better check the other side then."

Mac would never forget the last time he had seen Mike's backside. He wept for him then and the tears were there again looking at the perfection of his little boy bottom, all pink and round. He had to lighten this or he was going to make a fool of himself. He slapped the cheeks gently and spoke.

"You still look perfect, Tiger, a gay man's dream I guess."

Mike rolled back over and covered himself.

"I want to be like you when I get out of here, Mac. Will you teach me all the manly activities so that I am never taken for a nerd or wimpy kid again?"

"We are going to do whatever you want when we get you out of here. Are you going to college?"

"No Mac, I've decided I'm going to do courses on the internet to fit in to what I want to do with my life. I don't need a degree because I'm never going to need to go for a job interview. I'll fit into Mum's business wherever I feel comfortable. I love my music, and I'll probably always love to study birds, but I know I am going to be an incredibly wealthy man one day. It would be irresponsible not to prepare for it. It was different with my biological father, he never wanted me, he wanted a clone of him. Mum and you want me, and I'm happy with that."

Mike came out of the clinic and to the doctors amazement there was no body damage at all. Psychologically they were not sure, but he didn't appear to have any problems, if there were any they would probably surface when he tried sex for the first time. The shrinks knew that he was a passive gay man, and that his lover had also been his abductor. They had seen the video of his multiple rape by the ten monster cocks, but, he appeared to have shrugged that all off.

One month later, he gave his mother's hand in marriage to the man he almost worshipped.

When they returned from honeymoon, Maria began to think she had lost her son for a second time, and her second husband as well. The two men did everything together.

"Are you sure you love me Mac, and haven't just married me so that you can have Michael?"

Mac looked shocked until he saw the little grin spread across her face.

"Mmm, well, you have to admit he is an absolutely beautiful young man."

He grinned as well then.

"I'm sorry my love, I promise I'll spend more time with you."

Maria shook her head.

"No you won't, I wasn't serious. I am so happy to have two beautiful men to smile for and know that they both love me as well as each other. Seriously Mac, has Michael said anything about sex since he came out of hospital?"

Mac shook his head, "No and I'm not going to raise the subject. Let him come to terms with that subject in his own time."

Chapter 5

It had been a year since Mike's release from the clinic. Mac had been teaching him the art of self-defense, and he was good. He had also learnt to ride, shoot, sail, orienteer and he was the holder of a private pilot's license. He had spent time with his mother learning about the business and flown with her and Mac on visits to her global network of companies. On the flights he had spent more time in the co-pilot seat than the co-pilot did, and the aircraft spent more time manual handling than it did on auto-pilot. Mac and Maria never complained at some of the slightly uncomfortable maneuvers or the occasional hard landing. The captain always looked slightly pained as he apologized to Maria on these occasions.

"Captain I expect you made the odd landing a little too firmly when you were learning. As long as Michael doesn't tell me you handled ones like we have just experienced I don't suppose we are going to worry too much."

Mike would look suitably contrite on those occasions until Mac hugged him and made comments like, "We must think of a gentler way for you to wake us up, Tiger," always said with a smile.

The first sign of trouble in Paradise came one day in the gym at the house where Mac was teaching Mike wrestling moves. Mike sprung a boner while he and Mac were in close combat. Mac felt it and looked a little surprised into Mike's eyes. There were tears there as he returned the look.

"I love you Mac, I love you so much in a way that I know can't be. I am scared of trying to find a new lover, but I know I want to feel a warm body in my bed at night, and I guess that will mean sex. Please Mac, take me, make love to me just once so that I know I am whole again as a lover and won't chicken out at an important moment. I swear I will never ask you to do it again however good it is."

Mac was shocked into silence. He just looked at this boy that he loved like a son. He saw the uncertainty in his face and almost on impulse leant in and gave him a gentle kiss on the lips.

"I love you too Tiger, but you know this has thrown me a bit. Will you give me time to think about a reply?"

Mike smiled, "Of course, Dad, I didn't expect you to do it now, this instant."

Mac picked up that the boy obviously thought it was going to happen.

Talk with Maria that night was interesting. Mac told her word for word the conversation and what had caused it.

Maria surprised him.

"Are you going to?"

Mac looked at her as though she were mad.

"Of course not, but my worry is, what will Mike do if I don't. I can't condemn him to a celibate life, but he thinks that if I don't have anal intercourse with him that he will never dare get into a relationship. How about if I pay for an escort to take him to bed. Would he go for that, do you think?"

"Mac, Michael loves you as much as I do. He doesn't do anything now unless you have cleared it with him or sanctioned it. I hope he will become more of his own man but I think that to achieve that he will need your blessing in the only way he knows, doing it with you first."

Mac gulped, "This is crazy. What kind of a family are we? My wife sanctioning me having sex with her son."

"He is our son, and you know without asking the question. You have to do it Mac, and you will do so with my blessing."

Mac didn't sleep at all that night, and the next morning at breakfast he looked hunted. Mike looked worried.

"Don't worry Darling, just give your father time to work his head round this one. What are you both going to do today?"

"I think I'm going to come into work with you Mum, give Mac a break from me."

"I suppose I'd better do some work as well. Tommy will start thinking he's the boss soon if I don't show my face occasionally. And you two are going to be the death of me."

Mac stomped off and went into the offices by himself, driving his Lamborghini like a boy racer. He spent time with Tommy, bringing himself up to date and sorting a few problems before retiring to his office to think about Michael.

The boy was his mother's son, of that there was no doubt. He had all the good bits of her including her personality. More importantly for this scenario, he had her beauty, but in a masculine way. Could he make love to the boy? What would it entail? He guessed a lot of foreplay involving sucking his cock before opening up his anus and fucking him. That would be or could be the same as making love to a woman. The cock and rear entry would make it different, but not that much from the action side, well, the cock would be a major difference, but! He had been sucked so he knew what he liked, he would just have to do the same to Mike. He went to the internet for details about anal intercourse and thought he could handle it without traumatizing the boy. Kissing him wouldn't be too difficult, he didn't think, he loved the boy so it wasn't as though he was going to be kissing a strange male. Finally he knew he would have to appear enthusiastic or that would hurt him.

Maria made the decision easier for him.

"Darling, I have to go to LA for a couple of days. There is no point in dragging you with me. I'm going tomorrow and I'll be away one night."

Mac was sure this was a set up but he couldn't bring himself to accuse her.

The next morning, case packed, Maria kissed her two men and made it clear to Mac that if he did anything it was with her blessing.

"Mike, I'd like you here tonight for dinner and for the evening."

Mike walked across the kitchen and with no sign of nervousness, kissed Mac on the lips.

"I'd like that as well Dad. Can you ask cook to make it a special one?"

Mac knew then that Michael had decided it was a go with his mother's blessing, and Mike confirmed it with his next words.

"You must both love me more than I thought and probably more than I deserve."

"Never, you are everything I could wish for in a son. You have brought more sunshine into my life than I ever thought I deserved or expected. You brought me love that I never expected to find in a child and your mother added to it as we became friends and then lovers."

"I have a business tutorial at college today, but I'll be home late afternoon. Can we go for a ride before dinner?" Mike laughed then, "On horseback that is."

"Get out of here you little wretch or I'll be forced to spank you."

"Mmm, will you save that for tonight?"

He shot out of the door then, just in case.

Mac had a miserable day. Torn between his rank heterosexuality and the love he had for his son.

Mike arrived home full of the joys of life. He kissed Mac lightly on the lips.

"I can always do that in private to show you how much I love you can't I?"

The look on his face made the answer automatic for Mac.

"Of course you can. I love you too, and you are the only man that has ever done that to me, or ever will."

They both changed for riding and walked down to the stables, Mike chattering away happily about his day. They had a good workout on the horses before returning to the house.

"Mike, before you shower I want you to have a douche, or more as necessary."

Michael looked a little frightened.

"You know why, don't you?"

Mike nodded.

"A precaution, that's all. We don't go any further than you are comfortable with but we aren't going to risk anything unwanted either."

Tears in his eyes, Mike moved in close and gave Mac another kiss.

"I love you so much. I'm always amazed how gentle you are with me knowing some of the things you have done in your life."

Mac said nothing as the boy turned and went to his suite. He went to his and did the same.

'I'm not planning to let him enter me, but if he wants to then I'm not going to make a fuss about it,' was his thought as he dropped his riding clothes into the laundry basket.

Dinner was as good as it gets. Mac had told chef it was to be made up of Michael's favorite dishes and he chilled just one bottle of

Puligney Montrachet. He thought a couple of glasses each would not be detrimental to their performance in bed.

Dinner conversation was amusing as Michael did everything he could to skirt round the after dinner activity.

"I think that if you and I are still friends by breakfast time that we should check your mother's diary and find a few days when she is away again to go up to the cabin and maybe do a little hunting and fishing."

Mac smiled and Mike picked up on it.

"I think by breakfast time we will be a little more than friends."

He looked and sounded relaxed as he said it and Mac was pleased. He was nervous, which was a rare feeling for him, but he was determined that if this was what was required to make Mike whole again he would be the best gay lover he could be.

Mac always liked to pick up on the world news daily, so after dinner they sat in the lounge with coffees and watched it unfold.

"Nothing very thrilling there, Tiger, shall we go and make our own news?"

Mike nodded and they walked up to the master guest suite. Mac had already put lubricant on the bedside cabinet, removed the bed covers and adjusted the lighting to make it look more romantic.

"Neutral territory, Mike."

Mike understood why without explanations being necessary.

"Will you undress me Mac, and then let me undress you?"

Mac nodded and moved in close to his son. Shirt unbuttoned, and as he slid it off Mike's shoulders he planted a gentle kiss on his lips. Letting it slide to the floor, Mac dropped his head enough to kiss each of Michael's nipples. The boy gasped. Mac knelt on the floor then to remove shoes and socks before sliding his hands up Michael's legs to his waist band and unclipping his trousers, zip down and because the trousers were close fitting Mac had to help them over the hips before they dropped, revealing a pair of the new Japanese designer underwear, very brief and very sexy.

Mac sat back and scoped out the boy, thoroughly, having not seen him like this since his last day in hospital.

"You are quite the most stunning young man I have ever seen Mike."

What he was looking at was the same Mike of a year ago, but with one year of considerable physical activity and gym work.

He leant back in and kissed along Mike's tummy just above the waist band of the briefs, stroking the insides of the thighs as he did so. Mike very quickly came to full erection and Mac smiled as he eased the waist band over the rampantly hard cock and eased the briefs to the floor before indicating for Mike to let him remove them completely. He stood up then and looking in Mike's eyes, almost whispered.

"You are beautiful."

Mike blushed but his heart sang with pleasure after that comment. He then carried out the same action on Mac who wasn't erect when he had finished so Mike looked up at him as he took Mac's soft cock into his mouth. A look of surprise, a gasp of pleasure, and then a smile. Mike saw it and smiled as well, using a hand to play with Mac's balls and the other to maneuver the cock so that he could lick it all over. The stimulus didn't take Mac long to reach a very solid erection, the boy was good. Mike gasped as he sat back on his haunches to look.

"Oh God, Mac, that is so big. You will be gentle with me won't you?"

Mac lifted the boy to his feet.

"Have I ever been anything else with you?"

He shook his head, too overcome to speak, and then Mac pulled them close together to kiss the boy quite passionately on the lips.

"I love you Mike, you have brought me nothing but joy since I met you, now I hope to do the same for you."

There were tears in Michael's eyes as Mac laid him gently on the bed.

Mac knew what to do now, at least the first bit. Lips to start, then neck and slowly down to the nipples. He licked one and used his thumb to excite the other, then he nibbled them alternately until they were very hard. Hands first followed by the lips, he reached Mike's penis. He had never done this to another male, but having played with his own for the years when female company was non-existent, he knew exactly what to do to give his boy pleasure, and pleasure he gave. Sucking it was such an alien thought, but when he actually took the glans in his mouth and swabbed it with his tongue he was amazed how thrilling it felt. He sucked in more each time he bobbed up and down on it while he used a hand to massage the balls. He began to wonder who was getting the most enjoyment from his actions. Mike was such a masculine looking boy now, but at the same time there was so much of his mother in him that Mac felt totally at ease. He felt Mike's excitement so he moved back from the balls and stroked the perineum before letting a finger move gently over the anus. He felt Mike tense up and he moved back to the perineum and the balls. More stroking and he slid back to the anus again. This time he had the finger slicked up with his spit and Mike accepted the touch with no tensing. Mac had a serious problem now. He thought that Mike would love to have his arse licked, research had told him that a tongue across the anal entry was very thrilling, and this might make it easier for Mike to accept penetration. The idea was disgusting, but he knew Mike was very clean, and he smelt clean as well so he took the plunge and ran his tongue across the anus. He heard Mike gasp and speak soon after.

"Oh Mac, that feels like heaven."

Mac smiled then and licked Mike quite hard before using a hand to spread him a little more and prod the hole with his tongue. Mike came then in a gut wrenching orgasm spraying most of it over Mac's chest.

"Please don't stop, Mac, I want you so much."

Slicked finger again but this one eased into Mike. Mike's sphincter gripped him hard but he left his finger there waiting to see if Mike relaxed.

"That feels so good Mac, please don't stop."

Mac knew about the prostate, but his only experience with his own was at his regular medical checks. The doctor always checked it and he knew that his was very sensitive, even so, he had never been tempted to stimulate himself. Now he intended to excite Mike's. He found it near the limit of his finger penetration and Mike nearly hit the roof.

"Oh fuck, that feels so good."

Mac sniggered, Mike's comment had been made with such feeling.

Three fingers later, Mike was begging Mac to fuck him.

More gel than was really necessary on his cock and Mac eased some into Mike as well. He was between the boy's legs, which were spread wide and bent back. He had seen Michael like that once before, on the day of the multiple rape. Tears came to his eyes thinking about

"I think we can manage that. Like to go and clean up and clean your teeth. Back here when you're done."

Michael hopped out of bed but stood facing Mac for a minute noting his dad running his eyes over his whole body before settling on his eyes.

"You know it wouldn't be difficult to make love to you again, you are quite stunning and as beautiful in your masculinity as your mother is in her femininity."

Michael knew what Mac was saying, but it would be the weirdest setup in the world if it happened, his step dad making love to him and his mother.

Back in bed, Michael snuggled into Mac feeling his cock wedged in the crack of his ass. Mac cuddled him and kissed his neck.

"Sleep well my lovely boy."

When Mike woke the next morning he was alone in the bed. He felt Mac's side which was cold. He found him sat at the breakfast bar with a coffee and the newspapers. Looking very shy he spoke.

"Good morning, Dad."

Mac didn't miss the change of address. He was no longer Mac.

"Good morning, Son."

Huge grin on his face.

"I love you Dad."

Mac grinned as well, "And I love you too. I guess you know your mother does as well or she would never have permitted this."

Mike blushed.

"I know, and I'll try to pay both of you back by never disappointing you."

"I doubt that will happen, but it is good to hear it spoken."

Mike stayed home that day working on assignments and Mac went into the office. He arrived back home as Maria's limo dropped her at the front entrance. They walked into the house together and Maria's first question nearly floored Mac.

"Do you want a divorce now, but continue to live here as my son's lover?"

Mac looked at her as though she were mad. He was spared an answer as Michael burst into the entrance hall and grabbed his mother in a hug that nearly broke her ribs.

"Thank you Mum, I love you more than anyone else in the world."

Maria smiled.

"That's good to hear, so I can have my husband back, can I?"

Michael looked a little bemused.

"I assume that you found out one of the reasons that I love this big lug."

Michael's grin now almost split his face in two.

"Big lug is the last thing I would call him. He is absolutely the most incredible lover a man could ever wish for. How can you ever let him out of your bed?"

Mother and son were laughing so much they had to hold each other up.

Mac looked disgusted, well he tried to.

"I don't believe this and I doubt anyone else in the world would either. My wife and my son discussing my merits as a lover."

That made matters even worse, mother and son were almost hysterical. Mac stomped off trying very hard to look angry. He made it to the study before he nearly fell over as well laughing.

Epilogue

Ten years later.

Maria walked into the breakfast room.

"Good morning, Darling. How are you today?"

"Morning, Mum. Good as always. Charles and I both have early meetings today so we'll be in the office before you."

"Good morning to you too Charles, I see my son is still the slave driver."

"Yes, he is. If I didn't love him so much I'd look for another job with a human for a boss instead of this machine."

Michael laughed.

"That wasn't what you said in bed last night."

Maria laughed. "TMI, Michael Connors."

Three happy laughing people greeted Mac as he walked in, also dressed for the office.

"Mmm, three laughing senior executives, I have to assume Connors International hasn't gone bankrupt overnight."

Michael looked suitably proud as he spoke to his father.

"Better than that, Dad. Charles and I are going in early to meet the company lawyers. We should be signing the contracts to take over all of Global Media's African companies today."

Of course Mac knew that. He was after all Senior Vice President of Connors Int'l. It was however Michael and Charles jointly who had negotiated a first class deal. Michael's biological father had very little choice but to agree terms. Through nominee accounts, Connors had been buying Global Africa's shares for the last two years. When African economies faltered and the shares came on the market Michael's people had bought them and without realising it Noel had lost control of his companies to his son.

Michael turned the screw at the first face to face he had with his father since before his kidnapping.

"I don't really think I need to waste any more of my time here Mr. Harris, I'm sure my assistant can tie up any loose ends."

With that Mike walked out. Petty, but incredibly satisfying. His father, he knew was the same age as Mac, but Mac looked a good fifteen years younger.

'You could have had all the love and affection that has kept Mac young, if you hadn't been such an asshole,' was Michael's thought as he walked along Wall St. whistling a happy tune. He and Charles had been doing everything together for years, ever since they met at the company's head office when Michael started working with his mother and Mac. It wasn't exactly love at first sight, but they had found that they had so many interests in common that their friendship grew.

Mike sniggered about it when he remembered how it had become sexual. Exactly the same as it had with Mac. They had been wrestling during one of their workouts and Charles had sprung a boner, and what a boner. Mike had been mouth agape when they had pulled apart and he had looked down at Charles groin.

"Oh my God, that is amazing. Did I cause that?"

Charles looked as though he was going to faint, he was blushing almost purple.

"I am most awfully sorry. I'll tender my resignation to your mother immediately."

Mike had looked bemused.

"Whatever for, I am so flattered."

Charles's turn.

"But I'm a faggot."

"Oh Chas, that is such an awful word. You are gay, and you should be proud of it."

"I don't understand."

Michael just grinned.

"It doesn't matter, I'll try to explain in bed if you will come home with me and fuck my brains out with that lethal weapon you have between your legs."

Charles did just that showing Michael love making that he had only experienced once before in his life.

Lying back in his bed after they had finished Michael spoke.

"Only one man has ever come close to making love to me with so much passion. I never thought to see him bettered, but you have today, Chas. Will you be my boyfriend?"

Charles had grinned and a couple of months later had moved in with Michael. A year after that, Mac and Maria had become Mum and Dad. Now they were both Vice Presidents in charge of acquisitions. Connors Inc. had gone from strength to strength under Mac and Maria, gradually adding Michael and Charles to the top team.

Charles' love for Michael had grown exponentially during their ten years together and the dual love had led to both men exceeding their own expectations.

Michael never became a concert pianist but he did give the family and selected guests incredible enjoyment from his playing.

Charles talent was on horseback and they rode together frequently, but it was on the polo field that Mike's eyes shone the brightest as he watched Charles' fine display of horsemanship. The stables were full of polo ponies, Mac's present to Charles after he closed an incredibly lucrative deal for the company.

No one in the Connors household ever mentioned the kidnapping, but Michael had told Charles at the beginning of their relationship. He had, however never told him who the other incredible lover was. That was one family secret that he would carry to his grave.

~~The End~~

Watch out for Dexter Chase's next book:

Read the sample in the next page>>>

"What's your name, boy?" I said, looking at the white boy.

"I'm Abraham."

"Well Abraham, in this house you'll be called Abe and you'll be punished if you ever talk to me again without addressing me as 'Sir.' Do you understand?"

He looked a little terrified but answered me correctly, "Yes, Sir."

"And what about you?" I said, looking at the black man.

"I'm Zeke ----------- Sir."

I smiled at the long pause before the 'Sir' came out.

"Alright Zeke and Abe, I want you to put your hands on your sides and then turn around slowly for me until I tell you to stop."

They looked at me a little oddly before complying. When I was satisfied, after I had them both imprinted in my brain, I told them to stop and started questioning them.

Abe was eighteen, an illegal resident who had outstayed his visa. Zeke was a local, twenty-two years old, too lazy to work so took to crime. Both were well put together physically and during the next six months would look even better. My property was a working estate, producing good quality tobacco. I staffed it with local labor and treated them well, but Abe and Zeke would be treated as slaves. I told my overseer to do the same when they were working with him.

"Now, I want you both to get erections so that I can see what I'm going to be playing with for the next six months."

Abe looked shocked, Zeke looked belligerent, neither moved until I picked up the controller again, then they set to with Abe blushing and Zeke whining that this wasn't right.

Job done and I noticed Abe's cock first. It was interesting. Uncut, but when he pulled his skin back it looked circumcised, about six inches long. It was pretty like the rest of him with his medium-length, fair hair and blue eyes. Zeke took my breath away and made Abe's eyes come out on organ stops when he saw it. It was about twelve inches long, with nice thickness, and rigid. Both had pleasant ball sacs that I knew I would take pleasure in playing with. I was going to question them about their sexuality but not together.

Accommodation was the next thing to think about. Most of my workers lived with their families in the nearby village. The few that lived on the plantation had comfortable accommodation in a block close to the main gate so that they could wander into the village without a long walk. The only place I could put my two slaves was in a woodshed behind the house which was off to one side among the trees. I made them clean it out then we brought up two spare beds from the workers' block and I connected a hose to the water spigot.

"You'll eat in the kitchen of the main house except when you are working with the field gangs. If you give cook any trouble, I'll banish you to your shed and you'll eat the scraps that cook would normally throw away. You will always be with the working gang or in your shed unless I tell you otherwise, except of course for your meals. Disobey me and you will suffer the consequences that I can assure you will be very painful. Also, you will remain naked at all times."

That last one got the response I expected from Zeke. So, purely out of annoyance, I zapped him again with a 3. It soon became clear to me that Abe was in this position because he was easily led and had become a natural subservient to Zeke's demands. That however didn't result in any sexual contact, I found out later.

Both young men appeared to be heterosexual, but in Abe's case was a perception rather than something he had tried. Zeke boasted of his exploits with the ladies and I took it with a pinch of salt. What I decided though was that Abe was going to fuck Zeke first. I intended to have both of them frequently and provided that Zeke became less aggressive and more compliant, I wanted to feel his monster in my love tunnel sometime. It looked amazing.

Purchase **Caribbean Fun by Dexter Chase** in
Amazon.com ☺ Available soon…

Also by this Author:

Mastered

Go For Goal Or… Guy?

Ruin

The Loser

Forced by the Military

Lucifer's Academy

So Full It Hurts!

Bully to Slave

Play & Pretend

The Submissive Bad Boy

Unexpected Island Mates

No Hoper

From the Author

If you enjoyed any of my books then please share the love and click like on my books in Amazon.

If you write me a review and send me an email I will send you a free book, or many.
(Just know that these emails are filtered by my publisher.)

Good news is always welcome.

One Last Thing, For Kindle Readers...

When you turn the page, Kindle will give you the opportunity to rate this book and share your thoughts on Facebook and Twitter. If you enjoyed my writings, would you please take a few seconds to let your friends know about it? Because... when they enjoy they will be grateful to you and so will I.

Thank You!

Dexter Chase
dexter_chase@awesomeauthors.org

About the Author

Dexter Chase is a writer of hot, gay erotica stories in both paperback and Kindle versions.

His very first book published is **Mastered (Sensual Tales from Ancient Egypt)** which is about an eighteen-year old Ajax, who was taken as a slave and brought to a great house by a high-ranking soldier.

Check out his books and you'll enjoy extreme gay erotica of all time.

www.ingramcontent.com/pod-product-compliance
Lightning Source LLC
Chambersburg PA
CBHW061456170626
46811CB00004B/1538